Frank Bolles

Chocorua's Tenants

Frank Bolles

Chocorua's Tenants

ISBN/EAN: 9783743303447

Manufactured in Europe, USA, Canada, Australia, Japa

Cover: Foto ©Andreas Hilbeck / pixelio.de

Manufactured and distributed by brebook publishing software
(www.brebook.com)

Frank Bolles

Chocorua's Tenants

" Westward of Chocorua water "   (Page 57)

CHOCORUA'S TENANTS

BY

FRANK BOLLES

BOSTON AND NEW YORK
HOUGHTON, MIFFLIN AND COMPANY
The Riverside Press, Cambridge
1895

The Riverside Press, Cambridge, Mass., U. S. A.
Electrotyped and Printed by H. O. Houghton & Co.

CONTENTS

LIST OF ILLUSTRATIONS

CHOCORUA'S TENANTS

THE CROW

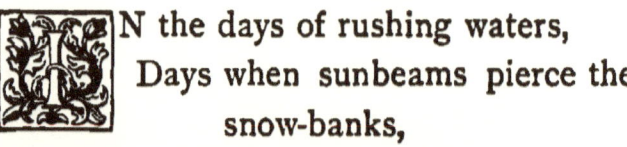N the days of rushing waters,
    Days when sunbeams pierce the
        snow-banks,
Days when maple sap is moving,
Days when on the lake's broad surface
Dark and spongy grows the ice-field,
From his range beside the ocean,
Longing glances towards the mountains
Darts the crow with thoughts of nesting.

High and higher climbs the Sun king,
Hurling burning darts before him
Into dark and frozen valleys,
Into cold and silent forests.
Then the crow on Scarborough marshes

Hears the laughter of the waters,
Hears the groaning of the ice floes,
Hears the rush of Piscatáqua ;
Hearing, soars on high exulting,
Beats his wings against the west wind,
Seeks Chocorua and his nesting.

In the orchard sings the bluebird ;
In the forest mews the red hawk ;
Butterflies, from winter slumbers,
Flutter o'er the wasting snow-drifts ;
Then it is a distant cawing,
Growing louder — coming nearer,
Tells of crows returning inland
From their winter on the marshes.

Iridescent is their plumage,
Loud their voices, bold their clamor,
In the pools and shallows wading ;
Or in overflowing meadows
Searching for the waste of winter —
Scraps and berries freed by thawing.

Weird their notes, and hoarse their croak-
    ing ;
Silent only when the night comes.

Where Chocorua water ripples
In its first half-conscious struggle
From its mother-mountain parting,
On its journey seaward starting,
Rises high a grove of pine-trees.
Graceful are they as the feathers
Bound about a chieftain's temples ;
Graceful as the slender fern fronds
Swayed by every passing wind-breath.

In these pines the crows have nested
Countless seasons.   From their branches
Robber leaders, full of bluster,
Forth have led their black marauders
To the ploughings, to the corn-fields,
To their battles with the farmer.
High above the singing water,
Anchored firm against the tempests,
Shrewdly screened from passing hunters,

Rest the nests of matted pine twigs,
Rest the castles of the robbers.

In the days of melting snow-drifts,
Days when down the lakes come drifting
Wreck and raft of winter's ice-field,
Crows are busy in the treetops.
Far away upon the hill crests,
Scanning lake, and road, and meadow,
Are the pickets, full of clamor.
If by chance they see the farmer,
Hills reëcho, and the pine-trees
Are deserted, left in silence.

When hepaticas are blooming,
When the blood - root smiles towards
      Heaven,
When young columbine the jester
Shakes her bells above the moss-cups,
Mother crows with warm devotion
Guard their eggs beneath their feathers,
Watch afar the farmer planting,
Count the days until the hatching.

" Deep within the forests' reaches "

Midway in the month of roses,
When beside the brook is blooming,
Pure and shy, the sweet linnæa ;
In the pines, among the beeches,
On the boulders, cawing, scolding,
All the crows in Crowlands gather.
Then it is the young are learning
How to stand and beat their pinions,
How to caw, and croak, and bluster.
Happy days those days in June-tide;
Days of feasting, days of plunder.

When the goldenrod uplifted
As a wayside benediction
Cheers the traveler on his journey
Through the sultry hours of August,
Deep within the forest's reaches,
In the shadow of the ledges,
Where the mosses drip with moisture,
Where the trout brook softly splashes,
Where the big-eyed flying squirrels
Undisturbed dream out the daylight,
Gather crows in friendly concourse.

Some upon the oaks' low branches,
Some upon the cool, damp mosses,
Some within the limpid waters
Wade and watch their black reflections.
All their notes are low and drowsy,
Muffled croaks, and guttural cawings,
All their motions speak contentment,
Tell of coolness, well-fed comfort.

When the sun toward Passaconway
Takes his downward course towards even-
       ing,
Crows are out again and stirring;
O'er the pines excited circling;
O'er the lake with straight flight flapping;
On the hilltops loudly cawing.
But as darkness from the valleys
Reaches out and clasps the mountains,
Shadows, heavy-winged and noiseless,
One by one, throb through the pine woods.
Crows are seeking sleep the restful;
Crows regain their roosts in silence.

Days wear on, and summer passes ;
Chilling winds pour down from Paugus ;
Gold and crimson deck the maples ;
Purple are the fox grape clusters ;
Blackened ferns droop o'er the meadows ;
Farmers homeward haul their harvest.
Then in Crowlands there is bustle,
Noise, excitement, and confusion.
Snowflakes flutter round Chocorua ;
Black flakes settle on the pastures.
Every stump and every boulder
Has its sable robber chieftain.
Thousands congregate and quarrel ;
Miles away the mountains hear them.
If perchance a hunter passes,
If the cattle, restless, straying,
Snap dead branches in the forest,
Up the throng flies, clouding heaven,
Nervous, petulant, expectant.

When the chill gusts sweep past Paugus,
Lashing all the lakes to white foam,
All the mighty hosts of Crowlands

Mount the air by common impulse ;
Turn their legions towards the eastward,
Turn their backs upon the mountains,
Turn away from threatened hunger ;
Seek the salty wastes of tide land,
Seek the boundless flats of Scarborough,
Seek the broad-winged gulls and gannets,
Seek the spoil of cruel Ocean.

Silent snows fall on Chocorua,
Snows which bury ledge and thicket.
In the pine grove all is quiet ;
Squirrels slumber in the crows' nests ;
Owls and foxes rule the forest ;
Days are short and nights are frozen.
Thus the winter broods o'er Crowlands
In the days when crows are absent.

THE LOG–COCK

IN the glens below Chocorua,
   In the forests north of Paugus,
   On the steeps of Passaconway,
Where the yellow birch and hemlock,
Scarred not by the blade of commerce,
Spring from moss-clad beds of granite ;
Where the brown bear, law defying,
And the red deer, law protected,
Make their homes among the moose-wood,
Sleep upon the sweet linnæa ;
Where in spring the leaping waters
Rush in three ways towards the ocean,
By the Saco, by the Bearcamp,
By the mad Pemigewasset ;
Where in winter moaning tempests
Rack the forests, whirl the snowflakes,
Dwells in grim and lonely glory,
All the year, the sombre log-cock.

Would you seek him ?   Borrow owl wings
Soft as darkness, light as lake-mist ;
Learn to tread the leaves with fox feet,
Like the hare to cross the snow-drifts,
Learn to burrow like the woodchuck,
Learn to listen like the partridge,
Learn to wait as does the wild cat,
Learn to start as does the red deer ;
Wary, watchful, is the log-cock,
Man among his foes most dreading.

Once his realm reached to the ocean,
Once the Saugus heard his clamor,
But the hand that felled the hemlock
Drove him backward to the mountains.
Seek him not beside still waters,
Seek him not in meadow grasses,
Seek him not in new-grown timber ;
Only in primeval forests,
Only where the mighty hemlocks
Skyward lift their storm-bent branches,
Will you find the log-cock toiling,
Will you hear his shriek appalling,
Will you see his flame crest gleaming.

In the early winter mornings,
Ere the crossbills leave the pine woods,
Ere the grosbeaks seek the ash seeds,
Ere the red polls find the birch buds,
Ere the titmouse calls his Phœbe;
While the red fox still is prowling,
While the partridge still is budding,
Just before the sun comes stealing
Upwards from the Bearcamp meadows,
You may hear the log-cock working
In the glens below Chocorua,
In the forests north of Paugus,
On the slopes of Passaconway.
Hammer blows on hollow tree-trunks,
Blows which echo from the mountains,
Strikes he with his nervous chisel.
Chips are flying all around him,
Chips [1] are piling high below him,
Still his blows fall fast and earnest,
Still the cliffs and woods repeat them.

[1] The writer, attracted by a pile of chips on the snow, once found a hole in a hemlock trunk recently dug by a pileated woodpecker, from which 268 cubic inches of wood had been removed.

If with fox feet you approach him,
If with scant breath you discern him,
In this early winter morning
As he toils with noisy rappings,
You will see his claws embedded
In the hemlock's outer fibre,
You will see his glossy plumage
Dark against the snowy hillside,
You will see his head thrown back-
          ward,
Then with spiteful force flung forward,
You will see the fresh chips flying,
You will hear the tree complaining.

If you crush the crust beneath you,
If his glance chance to be towards you,
You will see the flame crest lifted,
You will see his eye flash anger,
You will hear a shriek so vengeful,
In your dreams will come its echo.
Then the log-cock will have vanished,
And the ants within the hemlock
Will escape his morning drilling.

If with summer heat half-fainting
On Chocorua's slope you linger,
Ossipee and Tamworth water
In the distant sunbeams flashing,
Once again with sudden wonder
You may hear the log-cock's signal,
Weird, unearthly, fear inspiring.
To his mate, perhaps, a love note,
To their young in hollow tree-trunk
It may tell of tender morsels,
Found beneath the mouldering pine bark.

When the blade of greed and commerce
Robs the Saco of its woodland,
Strips the mad Pemigewasset
Of its sheltering birch and hemlock,
Fells from Ossipee to Paugus,
Bares the crest of Passaconway,
Then the log-cock too will vanish,
Seeking death or distant refuge,
Shunning man, the sure destroyer,
Man who wastes the ancient forests.

As few know him, few will miss him,
Yet the few will mourn his going,
For among Chocorua's tenants,
Oldest seems he of its vassals,
From some former age surviving ;
Left to guard the ancient hemlocks,
Left to wave his flaming signal,
Left to shriek his vengeful warning,
Left to be the last to perish
In the conquest of the forest.

" Ice and snow incase Chocorua "

THE RUFFED GROUSE

ICE and snow incase Chocorua,
    Ice and snow press down the
        forests,
Ice and snow enthrall the rivers,
Under ice and snow the lake groans,
Sends wild moanings to the mountains,
Tells its pain to gloomy Paugus,
Starts the deer on Passaconway.
Few and feeble are the sun's rays,
Coming late and going early,
Long the nights and chill their breathings,
Scant the song of birds in these days.

When the pallid sun has vanished
Under Osceola's ledges,
When the lengthening shadows mingle
In a sombre sea of twilight,

From the hemlocks in the hollow
Swift emerging comes the partridge ;
Not a sound betrays her starting,
Not a sound betrays her lighting
In the birches by the wayside,
In her favored place for budding.

When the twilight turns to darkness,
When the fox's bark is sounding,
From her buds the partridge hastens,
Seeks the soft snow by the hazels,
Burrows in its sheltering masses,
Burrows where no owl can find her.

Ah, how welcome is the springtime !
With its hoard of buds expanding,
With its berries left uncovered
By the melting of the snow-fields,
With its sweet, pure western breezes,
With the perfume of the mayflower,
With the singing of the finches,
With the music of the waters.

From the glens below Chocorua
Comes the sound of log-cocks drumming.
In the poplar groves of Paugus
Every downy beats his answer,
In the orchard and the birch wood
Joyous titmice plan their dwellings,
In the pine wood by the lake shore
Bustles back and forth the nuthatch.

Then it is the stately partridge
Spreads his ruff and mounts his rostrum,
Gazes proudly round the thicket,
Sounds his strange and muffled signal.
First with slow and heavy measure,
Then like eager, hurried heart-beats,
Ending in a nervous flutter
Faster than the ear can reckon.

Midway in the May-month season,
From her haughty, strutting master
To the silence of the pine wood
Steals the happy partridge mother,
Under cloak of yew and moose-wood,

Under brush and in the shadow,
Seeks a hollow lined with mosses,
Filled with leaves and sweet pine needles;
There her pale brown eggs she fondles,
There in anxious silence watches,
Stirs not, starts not, though dread danger
Passes near her, crashes by her.

Warm the leaves when chicks are hatch-
      ing,
Full the ground of dainty morsels,
Broad the ferns to hide her darlings,
Keen her ear to tell of danger.

If perchance a man approaches,
Nears her brood and notes her presence,
Ah, how quickly does the mother
Risk herself to save her nestlings!
Whining, moaning, near him crouching,
Limping, fluttering, leading onward,
While the chicks, with matchless cunning
Craft inherited from ages,
Under leaves, beneath broad mushrooms,

Into stumps, or gaping ledges
Crowd their downy, frightened bodies,
Wait till danger long has vanished.
Then with reassuring mewing
Comes the mother back to call them,
Nestle one by one beneath her,
Soothe their fright and preen their plum-
    age.

Anxious days — the days of autumn,
When from foggy morn till evening
Every mountain rolls back echoes,
Guns are thund'ring, dogs are yelping,
Danger lurks in every thicket,
Flocks are broken, broods are scattered.

Red the maples — red like heart's blood,
Thick the leaves fall — thick as sor-
    rows,
Every breeze becomes a warning,
Every creaking limb a terror,
Every trailing stem of blackb'ry
Seems a snare to seize the heedless.

High upon the oaks the squirrels
Frolic fast among the acorns,
On the moss beneath, the chipmunks
Gather up the falling treasures.
Shrill and nervous is their signal,
If their ever-watchful glances
Fall upon the skulking hunter
Prowling through the distant shadows.

When October sears the oak leaves
Silence settles on the forest.
Southward have the swallows darted,
Southward sped the warbler legions,
Southward are the thrushes flocking,
Crows complaining seek the Ocean.
With the snowflakes o'er the mountains
Hasten past the hawks from Northland,
Speed along the titmice, juncos,
White - crowned   sparrows,   wrens,   and
        creepers,
Tiny kinglets, sweet-voiced bluebirds,
All in eager search for havens
Where the touch of winter kills not.

Close behind them come the crossbills,
Come with joyous notes the redpolls,
Come pine grosbeaks, too confiding,
Come the hosts from Arctic nestings.

Colder grows the lengthening darkness,
Feebler grow the sun's caresses,
Wailing winds rush through the forests,
Sweeping myriad leaves before them ;
But the partridge fears no storm-wind,
Winter has for her no terrors.
Warm her heart and thick her feathers,
Strong her wings and brave her nature,
She exults in whirling beech leaves,
Groaning branches make her music,
Snowflakes form for her a shelter,
Food is certain as in summer,
Foes are fewer than in autumn.

Countless ages has Chocorua
Seen the partridge in the forest,
Heard his intermittent drumming,
Seen him budding night and morning.

May the ages still unnumbered,
While the mountain horn endureth,
Find the partridge near Chocorua
Joyous all the twelve-month season.

„ Cliffs below Chocorua's shadow "

THE EAVES SWALLOW

EARS before the Saco meadow
    Felt the feet of wand'ring white
        men,
Years before Chocorua's echoes
Were aroused by mimic thunder,
Mimic thunder from the rifles
Of the hunters, of the white men,
Cliffs along the face of Paugus,
Cliffs along the Saco valley,
Cliffs below Chocorua's shadow,
Bore the mud huts of the swallow.

Not the swallow of the sand-bank,
Not the swallow of the tree-trunk,
Not the swallow of the rafter,
Not the friendly purple martin,
Nor the swift which haunts the chimney,
But the swallow of the mud nest,

He with blue and chestnut breastplate,
He with snow upon his forehead.

From the mud-banks in the river
Pellets bore he to the cliff's face,
One by one he stuck them fast there,
Till his fortress was completed,
Arched and roofed and lined with fea-
        thers,
With its tube-shaped entrance pointing
Downward, so no rain could enter ;
Happy homes, those by the Saco,
Few the foes could reach their treasures.

By and by the Saco meadows
Felt the feet of wandering white men,
By and by Chocorua's echoes
Were awakened by the rifles,
By and by the stately pine woods
Helped to build the white man's home-
        stead,
By and by great barns were planted,
Milestones in the new-made clearings.

Then the swallows from the mud huts
Came to hover in the barnyards,
Hover round the strutting roosters,
Hover near the dreaming cattle ;
Feathers plucked they from the pullets,
Flies they caught above the heifers,
Mud they found beside the dug-outs,
Which contained the bright spring water
Led there from the upland ledges.

Rising high above the barnyards,
Like the cliffs above the Saco,
Were the weathered walls and shingles
Of the farmer's barns and lean-tos ;
Gray like rock, but warmer, drier,
Full of cracks and facing four ways,
Better surely for the mud huts
Than the dewy cliffs of Paugus.
So the builders of the mud huts
Left the meadows of the Saco,
Left the glistening cliffs of Paugus,
Came and dwelt beside the white man,
Built their huts beneath his barn eaves,

Won his love and kind protection,
Multiplied, and lived in plenty.

One by one green leaves turned crimson,
One by one the winters melted,
Years rolled on past men and swal-
    lows,
Both forgot that once the mud huts
On the Saco cliffs were plastered —
Barns alone were made to build on,
So young mothers taught their nestlings.

But with time the thrifty farmer
Learned that clapboards neatly lapping,
Covering all the rifts and gapings
In the walls which kept his cattle,
Made their stalls and mangers warmer,
Stopped the icy draughts of winter.
Then he learned that oils and pigments,
Daubed and rubbed upon his buildings,
Kept the mischief of the weather
From the clapboards, from the finish.

As the old barns fell to ruin,
New ones, raised to take their places,
Lacked the broad and generous shelter
Which the eaves had once afforded
To the owners of the mud huts,
To the swallows of the Saco.

Weary-winged, from distant Southlands,
In the spring have come the swallows,
Seeking hopefully their nestings,
Seeking eaves and sun-warmed barn sides;
Come and found the crackless clapboards,
Come and found ill-odored pigments,
Come and found new barns for old ones,
Come and found no eaves for shelter,
Come with joy and met with sorrow,
Seeking vainly for new barn sides
Changeless as the cliffs of Paugus.

Weary-winged the homeless swallows
Flutter on into the darkness —
Whither going? That they know not.
But 't is certain that the Saco,

That the lonely cliffs of Paugus,
That the steeps below Chocorua,
Do not bear their cosy dwellings.
Years ago, on man depending,
Mother swallows taught their nestlings
Barns alone are made to build on —
Barns have failed them, man betrayed
        them.

THE BLUE JAY

ROM among Chocorua's tenants,
  From among the birds of Crow-
    lands,
One in all eyes is a villain.
Loathed, detested, hated, dreaded,
Known to be a thief and ruffian,
Known to be a foul assassin,
Known to be a sneak and coward,
Hated doubly for his beauty.

Crows are open in marauding,
Crows are black and bold and bragging,
Owls confine their crimes to twilight
Or the hours of moonlit silence,
Hawks in highest heaven hover,
Soar in sight of all their victims,
None can charge them with deception,
All their crimes are deeds of daring.

Clad in blue with snow-white trimmings,
Clean and smooth in every feather,
Plumed and crested like a dandy,
Keen of vision, strong of muscle,
Shrewd in mimicry and dodging,
Knowing every copse and thicket,
Warm in snow and cool in summer,
Is the blue jay still a villain ?
Outlawed by all bird tribunals,
As a wretch disguised, he's branded,
Shunned by every feathered creature ;
Yet he prospers, man admires him.

Through the tedious months of winter
Round the corn-barn's step he lingers,
Boldly down among the poultry
Comes he to secure their kernels ;
Through the barb'ries, through the
        cedars,
Prowls he searching for their berries ;
In the spruces, in the hemlocks,
Cocoons from the bark detaching.

But so soon as in the Maytime
Eggs are laid and young are hatching,
Berries, buds, and worms rejecting,
Turns this scourge to sweeter morsels ;
Woe awaits the early songster
Whose uncovered nest he chances
To discover as he 's sneaking
Through the forest seeking plunder ;
Wise the nuthatch and the titmouse,
Wise the bluebird and the downy,
To conceal their nests in tree-trunks
Where this monster cannot find them ;
Ask the vireo what happens,
Ask the junco where her eggs are,
Ask the thrush and ask the robin
What assassin slew their young ones.

Hundreds perish in the season,
Egg and young of birds as useful
As their slayer is unfriendly
To the ways and plans of farmers.

Retribution sometimes follows
On the footsteps of this monster.
Crows will fly among the savins,
Search among the bristling branches,
Find the nests of roots and bark strips
Armed with barbs and twined with bram-
        bles,
Full of eggs or young just gaping —
Dainty morsels those for crows' tongues.
Harsh the clamor when the robber
Comes to find his own home wasted,
Wild the screams and fierce the anger,
Vain the flights around the nesting.

Man admires him for his feathers,
Loves to watch him in the winter
Boldly fly among the poultry,
Snatching golden kernels from them,
But his peers alone can judge him
Justly, clearly, on his merits.
One and all they call him outlaw,
Hate him, loathe him, fear him, spurn
        him.

Be his plumage light and dainty
He is cousin to the raven,
Near of kin is he to Corvus,
Black his heart, and black his kindred,
False his colors, false his nature.
All his beauty is delusion,
All his tricks are tricks of darkness;
Grim Chocorua through his cloud veil
Ever looks askance upon him.

THE OVEN-BIRD

N the hollows of the mountains,
   In the valleys spreading from
      them,
Stand the rustling broad-leaved forests,
Trees whose leaves are shed in autumn.

Underneath them lie the leaf beds,
Resting one upon another,
Laid there yearly by the storm winds ;
Pressed and smoothed by winter snow-
      drifts.

In the days of spring migrations,
Days when warbler hosts move northward,
To the forests, to the leaf beds,
Comes the tiny oven builder.

Daintily the leaves he tiptoes ;
Underneath them builds his oven,

"Trees whose leaves are shed in autumn"

Arched and framed with last year's oak
    leaves,
Roofed and walled against the raindrops.

Hour by hour his voice he raises,
Mingling with the red-eye's snatches,
Answering to the hermit's anthem ;
Rising — falling, like a wind breath.

Strange, ventriloquous his music,
Far away when close beside one ;
Near at hand when seeming distant ;
Weird — his plaintive accrescendo.

Teach us ! teach us ! is his asking,
Uttered to the Omnipresent :
Teach us ! teach us ! comes responsive
From the solemn listening forest.

When the whip-poor-will is clucking,
When the bats unfurl their canvas,
When dim twilight rules the forest,
Soaring towards the high stars' radiance

Far above the highest treetop,
Singing goes this sweet Accentor.

Noontide never sees this soaring,
Midday never hears this music,
Only at the hour of slumber,
Only once, as day is dying,
When the perils and the sorrows,
When the blessings and the raptures,
One and all have joined the finished,
Does this sweet-toned forest singer
Urge his wings towards endless ether,
Hover high a single moment
Pouring out his spirit's gladness
Toward the Source of life and being.

BLACK DOMINO: THE MARYLAND YELLOW-THROAT

WHISPERING rushes, bending grasses,
Purple orchids, mountain holly,
Meadow-rue and clustering alders
Lie beneath the morning dewdrops;
O'er the lake the mists are floating,
In the east the sun is rising,
From the forest calls the hermit,
In the pine-tops crows are cawing.
To the lake a sluggish brook flows —
Light canoes may thread its mazes,
O'er it hang the sweet wild roses,
In its banks are muskrat's tunnels.
From a bunch of stiff spiræa
Calls a voice with merry music,
Calls " good morrow " to the meadow,
Calls a welcome to the sunlight.

Merry music — joy betokens,
Show yourself, blithe morning singer.

Deeply set among the grass stems,
Woven on them, woven with them,
Arched and covered by their tresses,
Holding precious eggs, a nest lies.
In its secret depths the mother
Listens to her singing master,
Feels the sunlight warm the grasses,
Hears the breezes stir the rushes,
Hears the dragonfly in passing
Buzz his greeting to the turtle ;
Overhead she sees the dewdrops
Flash and glisten green and ruby,
Through the forest of the grasses
Sees a spider spinning, spinning,
Spinning snares for lace-winged insects,
Hanging nets for plump mosquitoes.
Once again she hears her master
Call " good morrow " to the meadow.
Merry music — joy betokens,
Show yourself, blithe morning singer.

See, an alder lightly waving,
See, the rushes near are nodding,
Something stirs beyond the sedges,
Something golden gleams behind them.
Now the leaves are gently parted
Just above the meadow's carpet,
And the joyous singer coyly
Makes his bow before the curtain.
How is this? A masquerader?
Come, sir, will you not uncover?
Do not hide that gold and ermine
Under domino of sable.

Gone so quickly! Through the grasses
Like a ray of sunshine glinting,
But beyond them for a parting,
Rises clear, alert, his greeting —
To the sunlight, to the meadow,
To the forest, to the mountain.
Merry music — joy betokens,
Fare thee well, blithe masquerader.

TWO SENTINELS

ONCE upon the slope of Paugus,
  Reaching out towards Passacon-
    way,
Grew a mighty hemlock forest.
Proud, aspiring, cloudland seeking ;
Through its branches swept the west wind,
Laughing, teasing, bent on frolic.
But the hemlocks would not heed it,
Stiffly held they high their summits,
Scorning mirth and jest and frolic,
Frowning on the roistering west wind.
Tapping, tapping on their shoulders
Came a friend from distant Northland ;
On his head a cap of yellow,
On his back a snow-white ladder,
All his form in sable gathered,
Brief his words, but full of warning :
" If you win the west wind's anger
Fear the days of late November."

From the vale of singing waters
Where the deer feed unmolested
Rise black Passaconway's ledges
Upward till the eye is dizzy.
Clouds around that summit linger,
Safe as in the high sky's pastures ;
Stars at night repose upon it,
Ere they seek their downward journey.
Years ago a dense spruce forest
Clung upon the heaped-up ledges,
Gained the resting-place of planets,
Reared itself into the cloudland.
Tapping, tapping on its shoulders
Came a friend from distant Northland ;
On his head a cap of yellow,
Round his form a cloak of sable,
Fingers three he raised in warning,
Brief his words but full of meaning :
" If you crowd upon the cloudland
Fear the days of late November."

One by one the days departed
To the land beyond the echoes,

One by one the nights departed
To the land beneath the shadows ;
Gone were birds and flowers and insects,
Silent was the piping hyla,
Sullen seemed the pushing west wind,
Dark and angry seemed the cloudland.
Then it was the wayward forests
Seemed to hear again the message —
" Fear the days of late November."

Night was resting on the heavens,
Not a star gleamed in the ether,
Only in the far-off Northland
Dimly glowed a lurid beacon,
Burning in the awful passes
Close by Carrigain the mighty.
Still the air, and soundless, heavy,
Phantom vapors mustered quickly,
Then a distant sound came booming
From the valley of the Saco,
Through the vale of singing waters,
Like a lake, ice-riven, moaning,
Like the sea in deep rock caverns,

Like an avalanche in winter,
Like the winds when ripe for rapine.
Louder, deeper, came the uproar,
Surging, leaping, came the cloud hosts;
Tremble now, presumptuous forests,
Winds and clouds combine against you,
Pitying stars have hid their faces,
Night with sinister intention
Ne'er was darker, never denser.
Woe, oh woe to you, proud forests,
Day shall dawn upon your ruin.
Ah, what sound is that of rending,
Crushing, crashing, splintering timber?
Hear the groans of breaking spruce trunks,
Hear the moans of straining fibres,
Hear the roar of falling boulders
Bounding down the endless ledges.
All of Passaconway's bulwarks
Seem to break before the storming.

Now the scene of battle varies —
Turning on the flank of Paugus,
All the hosts of wind and vapor
Crush their way across the hemlocks,

Leaving none to render witness
To the glory of their forest.

Morning dawned, and snowflakes fluttered
Millions deep upon the mountains,
Frozen tears of Nature's pity
Sent to hide the deed of darkness.
All the western slope of Paugus,
Passaconway's northern ledges,
Heaped with death were left dismantled,
Stripped of every form of beauty.

Years have passed, but still the mountains
Know the sentinels in sable.
When they tap the hemlock's shoulders
Terror thrills the broken forest.
Few their words and seldom spoken,
But when spoken full of meaning,
For to them the fall of forests
By the axe, or by the storm wind,
Means the loss of home and shelter,
Means extinction in the mountains
Which have been their border outposts
Since the red men trod the valleys.

THE PARULA

AR within the gloomy forest
    Stand the prophets of the swamp-
        land,
Tall are they, with storm-blanched fore-
    heads,
High they lift their arms towards heaven,
Moan when winds sweep chilling o'er them,
Weep when winter snows are falling.
Hanging loose in uncombed masses,
Downward trail their long gray beards.
Dismal owls abide beside them,
Bats and snakes and lizards haunt them,
In the night their feet are lighted
By earth's phosphorescent torches.

Years ago, in youth's keen vigor,
They were rulers of the forest ;
Far their leaf-hung limbs extended,
High their heads were held in sunlight,

But with age come fear and sorrow,
Memories of past misfortunes,
Pessimism, born of failures,
Half-healed wounds, bequests of folly.

Just as childhood romps and frolics
Heedless of complaining grandsires,
So around these swampland prophets,
While they groan and foretell tempests,
Dainty birds in summer hover.
In the moss-hung limbs they gather,
Rainbow-tinted, quick-winged warblers,
Heedless, joyous, evanescent.

In the trailing beards of gray moss,
Dainty hammock nests they tangle,
Weave them of the long gray fibres,
Line them with the softest meshes,
Leave within them precious treasures,
Tiny eggs, with rarest markings,
Tender, unprotected nestlings.

If by night the lightning flashes,
If from high Chocorua's ledges

Crashing thunder shakes the forests,
In their swinging nests the mothers
Cover close their downy darlings,
Listen startled to the groanings
Of the prophets, as they murmur,
" See — we told you — storms will dash
       you ;
Storms will crush you, rain will drown you."

When the sunlight greets the morning,
Safely swing the tiny hammocks,
And the gayly clad Parulas,
Flying through the dripping forests,
Sing aloud their joyous message,
" Nest we where no owl can find us,
Nest we where no hawk can see us,
Nest we where no jay can rob us,
Nest we where no feet can reach us."

But the prophets still will murmur,
Day and night, until the winter,
Night and day, until the summer,
On the folly of the warblers,
On the dangers of the swampland.

FOLLOWING the law of ages,
　　Law whose reason time half
　　　buries, —
Southward have the sparrows fluttered,
Southward have the finches hastened,
Southward have the juncos journeyed,
Southward, far beyond Monadnock.
They have seen the snow descending,
They have heard the ice king toiling,
They have listened to their elders
Saying — " Flee before the winter."

Ah, how silent are the forests !
Ah, how desolate Chocorua !
Listening ear can hear no music,
Yearning eye can see no color.
Hush — what sound was that from heaven
Sweet as chorus hymeneal ?

" Ah, how silent are the forests ! "

See — what falls from cloudland's spaces
Light of wing and warm of tinting ?
See, a host with song descending,
See, the snow with warm life dappled.

In the birches, on the grasses
Stiffly rising through the snow crust,
On the slope of yonder sand-bank
Where the snow has slipped and wasted,
Rest a flock of trustful strangers,
Lisping words of gentle greeting,
Rest and find the sun's rays warming,
Rest and find their food abundant,
Resting, sing of weary journeys
From a Northland cold and distant.

They can tell of Athabasca,
Of the land of Manitoba,
Of Mistassinnie, the wood lake,
Of the Saguenay's swift water ;
They can tell of boundless forests,
Rivers where the salmon plunges,
Lakes where wild geese dwell untroubled,

Heights where robber eagles linger,
Vales where caribou are feeding,
Glens in which at hour of evening
Rises wild disturbing clamor
From the lucivee, the wood fiend.

Rose-touched are their brows, with tints
        like
Lights upon a winter's snow-field,
Rosy are their caps as morning
When the storm clouds gather eastward,
Happy are their hearts and voices,
Happy are the fields and forests,
When their merry notes come jingling,
Sleighbell like, from upper ether,
Happy is the red-cheeked farmer
When they gather by his barnyard.

Even as the red-poll linnets
Gather from the bleaker Northland
On Chocorua's wintry pastures,
Scorned by sparrows, finches, juncos,
So in other scenes of world life

Cheerful hearts and rose-crowned fore-
    heads
Find the sympathy they search for
In the white, abandoned snow-fields,
In the silent, song-hushed pastures
Of some love-deserted soul-land.

MONK AND NUN: THE BLACK SNOW-BIRD AND WHITE-THROATED SPARROW

SK the lake to name her lover,
Ask, before the sun has risen,
Ask, before the breeze has wak-
    ened,
Ask, while yet within the waters
Dwells the image of the lover,
Tall and mighty, strong and rugged.
Did you hear a murmured answer?

Listen in the singing pine wood,
Listen, and a voice will bid you
Climb the ledges, struggle northward,
Find the red fox in his cavern,
Find the tittering groves of aspen,
Find the rushing mountain torrents,
Find the tangled vines and bushes,

Stand upon the mountain's shoulder,
Face the north wind, breast his jostling,
Call upon him for the answer.
Who is yonder fair lake's lover?

Will he tell you?   He will answer:
" In these spruces, on these ledges,
Dwell two spirits, born of music,
Creatures of the song and sunshine.
One in sombre cowl and cassock,
One with veil of snowy whiteness,
Both with voices full of sweetness.
They can tell you of the lover."

Then will pass the restless north wind
Through the humble bending spruces,
Leaving loneliness and mystery —
Sky so wide and earth so distant
Far below the trees are blended
Like sea waves on dim horizons ;
Lost in distance is the village,
Lost the hum of life and labor,
Lost the murmur of the river,

Lost the sense of human presence.
Close above the clouds are sailing,
Wafted out across the ether
From the peaks which guard the West-
land,
Towards the plain which holds the ocean.

Northward range on range of mountains,
Ragged-edged with balsam forests,
Stand like ranks of mighty soldiers
With their bayonets uplifted.
Hush! The north wind has departed,
Quiet reigns upon the mountain.
From the grove of spruces yonder
Comes a song of primal sweetness,
Every note is long and tender,
Held, drawn out, like words of part-
ing.
'T is the nun within her abbey
Singing of the life of virtue.
Hark! Beyond that riven boulder,
Poised upon the crag's steep border,
Rises heavenward a gloria.

"The crag's steep border"

Every note is full of gladness —
'T is the monk within his cloister
Pouring out his adoration.
Quickly ask them, ere the north wind
Comes again to mar the quiet,
Who it is that wooes the maiden,
Who may be the sweet lake's lover.
Ah !   What is it that they answer ?
Yes, they know but will not tell you.
Journey back into the valley,
Shun the red fox and the aspens,
Shun the tattling pines and north wind ;
Seek the lake herself at sunset,
Float upon her placid surface,
Look within her heart at twilight,
Ask her if she has a lover ?

Downward over thorny ledges,
Downward past the tittering aspens,
Heeding not the sneaking red fox,
Heeding not the tattling pine-trees,
Downward to the sandy margin
Whence with paddle swiftly plying,

Out upon the lake's broad surface,
Strong arms send the light boat flying.

Now the sun has met the forest,
Now the breeze has sighed and slumbered,
Now the whip-poor-will is calling,
Now at last the lake is placid.
Suddenly within the waters
Seems to grow a mighty figure,
Holding high an awful forehead,
Reaching far two arms of granite.
Ah ! they clasp the lake between them,
They enfold it, and the lover
Seems to fill the lake's whole being
With his beauty, with his power,
With his all-demanding presence.
So the answer to the question
Asked at dawn has come at twilight,
And the lake's mysterious lover
Is Chocorua, the mountain.

THE GREAT CRESTED FLY-CATCHER

ESTWARD of Chocorua water
Stands an ancient apple orchard,
Overhung by lofty maples,
Bearing scars of many sappings;
Warm and sunny is the orchard,
Plenty are its acid apples,
In its hollows squirrels nestle,
In its branches birds assemble.

Titmice love this orchard's hollows,
Caverns in its trunks and branches
Make them warm and cosy nestings,
Safely hidden from the blue jay.
Here the deer-eyed flying-squirrel,
Mice and bluebirds, swallows, adders,
Find in turn their favorite havens;
Here, as well, a harsh-voiced tyrant
Makes his home within a cavern.

Late in May he makes his nesting,
Seeks a deep and darksome hollow
In the orchard's oldest tree-trunk,
Lines it well with matted cow's hair,
Grasses, feathers, bits of wasps' nests,
Slender roots, or silky fibres,
Here and there a scrap of paper,
Shred of bark, or seed of thistle.

Odder things than these he uses, —
Things for something else than com-
      fort;
Sometimes to the general tangle
He will add a tail of chipmunk,
Sometimes fish scales, iridescent,
Mingle in the mystic chaos,
But his chiefly favored fetish
Is a piece of cast-off snake skin.

In this ill-assorted rubbish
Four or five strange eggs are hidden;
They are tinted like the matted
Leaves and grasses, hair and feathers;

From their larger end descending
Countless slender rays or streakings
Seek the point, while in beginning
They are blended in a tangle.

What can be the explanation
Of this bird's persistent fancy?
Why through countless generations
Have they sought for cast-off snake skins
To adorn or guard their nestings
In the hollow of the tree-trunks?
Do the mouse, the snake, and squirrel
Fear a scrap of harmless snake skin?

Wild and wary is this tyrant,
Harsh his screaming, angry whistle,
Strange his comings and his goings,
Strange his likings and his hatings;
Round about Chocorua water
He has found the haunts he fancies,
But in many another valley
None have ever heard his clamor.

He is one that shuns the winter,
Knows no home where snowflakes flutter.
Insect wings proclaim his coming,
Insect death foretells his going,
With the arbutus he enters,
With the goldenrod he passes,
Hither from the south in Maytime,
Thither with the equinoctial.

THE WHIP-POOR-WILL

OONLIGHT sparkles on the
water,
Breezes whisper in the aspens,
Foxes bark upon the ridges,
Owls complain within the forest,
Bats are flitting, crickets chirping,
Frogs in distant sedges croaking,
Muskrats in the weeds are splashing,
Mists across the lake are creeping.

From the clearing comes a message,
Tremulous and full of motive, —
Weird, half sorrowful, uncanny,
Taken up by other voices,
Echoed by the sleeping forests,
Borne across the lake's broad bosom,
Heard and answered by the herons,
Heard and answered by the divers.

Nearer comes the mystic singer,
Louder sounds the weird complaining,
Then a pair of soft wings flutter
Soundless, close above the bushes.
In the sand beside the lake shore
Drops the melancholy minstrel,
And again his lamentation,
Rhythmic, sad, with repetition,
Throbs across Chocorua water,
Echoes from the aspen forest.

In the sand the singer lingers,
Now and then a feline purring
Seems to tell of solaced sorrow ;
Not for long, for from his wallow
Comes the mournful repetition,
Broken by a gutt'ral clucking,
Sobbing to the wakeful echo.

Through the hours of moonlit darkness
Comes incessantly the message,
Now from shore, and now from forest,
Now from hill, and now from meadow,

" Sunlight sparkles on the water "

Sometimes sinking soon to silence,
Sometimes throbbing on till daylight
Reappears, and calls for quiet
Lest the sound throb on forever.

Sunlight sparkles on the water,
Breezes set the waves a-rolling,
Crows discourse upon the ridges,
Thrushes sing within the forest,
Swifts are flitting, sparrows chirping,
Cows in distant pastures lowing,
Minnows through the weeds are darting,
Clouds above the lake are sailing.

But the whip-poor-wills are silent;
In the copse, among the fern fronds,
Underneath the lady's slipper,
Voiceless, drowsy, hide the singers,
Hide so closely that no footfalls
Will arouse them, will disturb them,
Till themselves or eggs are threatened
By the foot of the invader.

THE KINGFISHER

HARK ! What sound disturbs the stillness
Of the forest, of the meadow?
Harsh the notes, a wild alarum,
Waking echoes from the ledges,
Mocking laughter from the hemlocks.
Hark ! it nearer comes and rattles,
Like the hail upon the grape leaves,
Like cold rain upon the cornfield.

From the clear Chocorua water
Slowly slips the wasting ice-sheet.
In the space reclaimed from winter
Pale blue skies are seen reflected,
And the sleeping lion's profile
From among them gleams majestic.

See, reflections calm are broken,
Waves arise and lap the ice-sheet,

And again the wild alarum
Echoes from the gloomy hemlocks.

From the agitated water,
Like a fragment of the picture
Of the April sky just broken,
Rises swiftly towards the forest
He who makes this clamorous discord,
He who broke the calm reflection,
Tyrant of the sleeping waters,
Terror of their finny dwellers.

Thus he comes with melting ice-sheets,
Comes with challenge and with bluster,
Flashing like a feathered arrow
Through the gleaming sun of Easter,
Searching for the schools of minnows
In the shallows, on the sand-bars,
Calling out his wild defiance
To the forest, to the mountain.

Weeks roll by, and May-time lingers,
Full of music, full of perfume.

Over eddying Bearcamp water
Myriad swallows glide and twitter.
Golden sand-banks flank the river,
Riddled are they, like a frigate
Wrecked by cruel grape and shrapnel,
Riddled by the swallows' borings.

Flash ! a jet of white and azure
Leaves the sand-bank, clips the water,
Rises to a blasted maple,
Drooping o'er the Bearcamp eddies.
Hark ! again the forest quivers
To the harsh and jarring challenge,
And again the fish are startled
By this plunge beneath the waters.

In the sand-bank, near the turf line,
Is a larger, deeper boring
Than the borings of the swallows.
Here the king's proud fisher lodges,
Lodges on a heap of fishbones,
Lodges in the deepest darkness,
Lays her seven snow-white treasures,
Fondles them and gives them being.

To the log-cock in the forest
Man's advances bring disaster;
To the phœbe and the bluebird
Farms are full of friendly shelter;
To the hawk the shotgun preaches,
Grouse the hunter keeps in peril,
But to this fierce water tyrant
All man's comings, stayings, goings,
Count for less than south wind whispers,
Count for nothing, pass unnoticed.
Proud, defiant, strong-winged, fearless,
All his daily needs supplied him,
Air and water, sand and fishes;
Given these and naught else needs he.

So he was in days unnumbered,
Days before man trod the forest,
Days before the thin ash-paddle
Cleft the waters of the Bearcamp;
Days when mighty glaciers, melting,
Made the lakes, which bred the rivers;
Days when great Chocorua's profile
Slept unknown beneath Arcturus.

So in some dim age of future
When man's foot has left these valleys,
This proud bird may still be monarch
Of the eddying Bearcamp waters.

www.ingramcontent.com/pod-product-compliance
Lightning Source LLC
Chambersburg PA
CBHW020041030726
47499CB00007B/2525